Every new generation of children is enthralled by the famous stories in our Well-Loved Tales series. Younger ones love to have the story read to them, and to examine each tiny detail of the full colour illustrations. Older children will enjoy the exciting stories in an easy-to-read text.

Tom Thumb

retold for easy reading
by VERNON MILLS

illustrated by JOHN DYKE

Ladybird Books Loughborough

There was once a woodsman and his wife who were very sad because they had no children.

"I wouldn't mind," said the wife, "even if we had just one child, but it's very lonely here when you are out all day."

"I know," said the woodsman. "It would be fine to have a youngster about the place."

"I wouldn't mind," said the wife, "if he were no bigger than my thumb. I just wish I could have a child to love and care for."

You can imagine how happy the couple were when sometime later their wish was granted, and they had a small son.

Strangely enough, he was no bigger than a man's thumb, and so they called him "Tom Thumb."

The woodsman and his wife fed young Tom on the best food they could buy, but he never grew any bigger. In spite of his size, he grew up to be a lively and clever young lad. They enjoyed having him to talk to, but couldn't see how he was ever going to be much help to them.

One day however his chance came.

"If only Tom were bigger," said the woodsman, "he could drive the horse and cart for me."

"I can, I can," cried young Tom.

"Don't be silly," said his mother. "You couldn't even hold the reins, and you would fall off the cart and be killed."

"If you will harness the horse, Mother, I will show you how I can drive it," said Tom.

"All right," said his mother, "but I don't see how you will do it."

Tom's father set off for the woods, whilst his mother harnessed the horse and put it into the shafts of the cart.

"Now my clever one, how are you going to drive this great thing?" Tom's mother asked.

"Put me into the horse's ear, and I can tell him when to start and stop. I shall be quite safe and warm in there. When I get to the woods, Father can lift me down," said Tom.

"Well," said his mother, "I'm not happy about it, but it will make a lot of difference to your father, so I suppose we must try it. Mind you are careful, and hold on tight over the rough tracks."

Off went the cart, with Tom tucked safely in the horse's ear. The horse did as he was told. When Tom said, "Faster," he strode out on the good parts of the road. When they came to rough tracks Tom said, "Steady boy," and the horse picked his way carefully over the rutted ground.

As they went along, they passed two men walking together. It happened that when the horse was close to the two men, Tom said "Steady, boy." The men were astonished to see a horse and cart without a driver. They were even more amazed to hear someone talking to the horse.

"Did you hear someone speak to the horse?" said one man to the other.

"Well, I thought I did," replied his friend, "but there's no driver and no one else in sight."

"Let's follow the horse and see if it happens again," said the first man.

So they followed the horse and cart into the forest and sure enough, they kept hearing someone talking to the horse. Eventually, the horse and cart came to the place where the woodsman was working.

" Hallo Father, I told you I could drive the cart for you," said Tom. " Will you take me out of here, please ? "

"Well done, Tom," said his father. "I didn't see how you were going to manage, but your clever idea certainly worked."

The woodsman carefully took Tom out of the horse's ear and sat him on his shoulder. Suddenly the two men realised how the horse had been going along without a driver. They also realised where the voice had come from.

"What a clever little chap that is," said
one of the men. "Will you sell him to us?
We will treat him well and look after him as
though he was our own child."

" But he is *my* child," said the woodsman, " and I wouldn't sell him for all the money in the world. Besides, his mother would be heartbroken. No, I cannot sell him. Be off with you."

Tom tugged at his father's ear and said in a whisper, " Let me go with them, Father, and take their money. I will slip away from them and be back with you in a day or two."

Reluctantly, the woodsman was persuaded, and sold Tom for a great deal of money. The men went away chuckling.

" We will take him from town to town and put him on show," said the first man. " That way, we shall soon make our fortune."

17

"Well, he won't cost us much," said his friend. "A little chap like that won't eat much, and he can travel in your pocket and sleep there at night."

So Tom travelled in the man's pocket, where he could look out and see the country-side as they passed. All day the men walked,

anxious to get to the next town. Towards evening, Tom called out to the man, " Put me down, please. My legs are cramped and I must stretch them." So the men stopped for a rest and put Tom down whilst they leant against a bank. Tom pretended to stretch his cramped legs but was really looking for somewhere to hide.

Suddenly Tom saw a rabbit hole in the bank and with a quick hop and a jump, stood in the entrance. "Goodbye, dear friends," he called. "Thank you for the ride. Next time, take more care! Little things get lost so easily!" With that, Tom disappeared down the rabbit hole at a run.

The men were furious. They poked into the hole with their sticks, peered down it and shouted, but all to no avail. Like most rabbit holes, this one had another entrance on the far side of the bank. Tom was soon out and struggling through the tall grass. The two men argued and complained and searched in vain along the bank. Soon it was too dark to see and they went on their way in a very bad temper.

Tom was glad to be free of the two men. Since it was now dark he looked round for somewhere safe to sleep. Stumbling back onto the path, he came across an empty shell. He soon curled up inside and was just falling asleep when he heard voices.

Two thieves were talking together. "How shall we manage to steal the parson's silver and gold?" said one to the other.

"I'll tell you," said Tom in a loud voice.

"Did you hear someone speak?" asked the second thief.

"Take me with you," said Tom, "and I will show you how to get the money."

The two men were puzzled. They could hear a voice, but they couldn't see anyone.

"Where are you?" asked the first man.

"Down on the ground," said Tom. "Follow my voice and you'll find me."

On hands and knees they searched and soon found Tom. Picking him up one said, "Whatever can a little chap like you do to help us?"

"I can get in between the bars of the window," said Tom, "and throw the money down to you."

"All right," said the men, "we'll take you with us and see what you can do."

When they came to the parson's house, Tom did as he had promised. Once inside the room he shouted, "Will you have all that's here?"

"Hush!" said the thieves, "you'll wake everyone up."

Tom pretended he couldn't hear them and shouted even louder, "How much do you want? Shall I throw it all out?"

The cook, who was sleeping in the next room, woke up, sat up in bed and listened.

The thieves, who had run away when Tom shouted, came back. "Stop shouting," they whispered, "and throw out the money."

Shouting as loud as he could, Tom called out, "All right, hold out your hands, here it comes."

The cook couldn't help hearing this and jumped out of bed. She ran to the door, but the thieves had run away. Whilst she went to fetch a candle, Tom escaped and made his way to the barn. He was tired and wanted somewhere to sleep.

The cook came back with the light and searched everywhere She couldn't find any-one. " I *must* have been dreaming," she said to herself, " and yet I swear I heard voices." Still puzzled, she put out the candle and went back to bed.

The hay in the barn was soft and warm. "I'll find my way home tomorrow," Tom thought. After all the excitement of the day he was soon fast asleep.

The cook was up early to feed and milk the cow. She went straight to the barn for some hay, and chose the very bundle that Tom was sleeping in to give it to the cow to eat.

Tom woke up to find himself being tossed about in the cow's mouth, and was nearly crushed between its great teeth. Suddenly he felt himself falling, and he landed in the cow's stomach amongst all the hay.

"It's very dark in here," Tom said unhappily, as he struggled to his feet. "There's not much room either."

As the cow ate, more and more hay came tumbling down and Tom was getting smothered. "Don't eat any more hay," he yelled as loudly as he could. "There's no more room down here!"

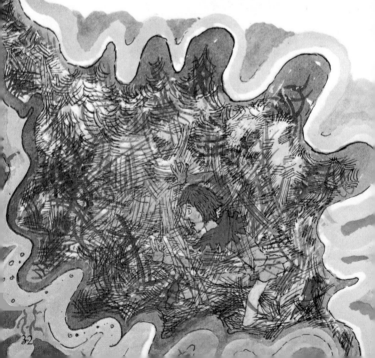

The cook was so startled to hear a voice coming from the cow's mouth that she dropped her bucket. Running back to the house, she called to the parson, " Sir, sir, the cow's talking!"

"You must be mad," said the parson, "Cows don't talk."

But just then Tom shouted again, "Don't eat any more hay, I can't breathe!"

The parson was sure the cow was bewitched and decided it would have to be killed.

After it was killed, the stomach, with Tom still inside, was thrown out into the yard. "Now is my chance," said Tom. "I must escape while I can."

He struggled and struggled until at last he got his head out into the fresh air. "Goodness, that's better," he said.

But his troubles weren't over. A hungry wolf passing by saw the stomach, snatched it up, and swallowed it at one gulp.

"Oh dear," said Tom, "here I am in trouble again."

Suddenly he had an idea.

"Wolf, wolf," Tom called, "are you still hungry?"

"I'm always hungry," said the wolf.

"Not far from here there's a house full of food you could eat," said Tom, and described his father's house and how to get to it.

"You can crawl through the drain into the kitchen," Tom said. "There's beef and ham and lots of other good things to eat there."

The wolf was very pleased at the thought of all that food. As soon as it was dark, he set off to find the house. When he got there he found the drain, crawled through it into the kitchen, and started to eat.

The wolf ate and ate until he was quite full.
Then he turned to go back through the drain,
but he had eaten so much that he was too
fat. He couldn't get out no matter how he
tried.

This was just what Tom had hoped would happen. He was so pleased his plan had worked that he started to shout and sing. "Be quiet!" said the wolf crossly. "You'll wake everyone in the house."

"I don't care," shouted Tom. "You've had *your* fun, now I'm having mine." And he shouted all the louder, and sang at the top of his voice.

The noise of Tom's singing and shouting woke the woodsman and his wife. They came to the door of the kitchen and opened it just a little.

The woodsman jumped back in alarm. "It's a wolf," he said to his wife, "and he seems very angry. I must fetch my axe."

Soon he came back with his axe, but his wife said, "What if the wolf gets past you? I must have a weapon too."

"Go and fetch the scythe then," said her husband. "When I hit the wolf on the head with the axe, you can cut him open with the scythe."

Tom had heard what his father said and was very frightened. As soon as he heard his parents come into the kitchen he shouted as loudly as he could, "Father, father, I'm here inside the wolf!"

The couple were amazed to hear their son's voice again after such a long time. "What can we do?" asked the wife. "If I cut the wolf open, I might kill the child."

"I'll kill the wolf with the axe," said the woodsman, "then we can get Tom out without any risk."

The woodsman cornered the wolf, and brought the axe down hard on its head. The wolf fell dead on the floor.

When the woodsman was sure the wolf was dead, he took his knife and carefully cut it open. Tom was delighted to be free once again, and his mother and father wept with joy to find him safe and sound.

"We didn't think we would ever see you again," said his mother, wiping away her tears. "What ever happened to you, and how did you come to be inside the wolf?"

"Start by telling us what happened to you after the two men took you off to the next town. You said you would escape and be back in a day or two," said his father.

45

Tom sat down on his mother's lap, and proceeded to tell them of all his adventures.

"Since I left you I have been in the strangest places," he said. "The first evening that the men took me away, I asked to be put down because my legs were cramped. When they weren't looking I ran into a rabbit hole and got away."

"Weren't you frightened," asked his mother, "all alone in the dark?"

"Not half as frightened as I was later," said Tom. "I pretended to help some thieves and ended up in a parson's house. Then the cook picked me up in a bundle of hay I was sleeping in, and I was eaten by the cow."

"However did you escape?" asked his mother.

"When I shouted, they thought the cow was bewitched and had it killed. I had just got my head out of its stomach, when the wolf came along and gobbled up the stomach with me still inside."

"It was a very clever plan to get the wolf to come in through the drain," said his father. "But it was just as well you shouted so loud, or we would have cut open the wolf with the scythe and you would have been killed too."

" Oh don't speak of it," cried his mother. " Now you are home again safe and sound we shall never sell you again, however much gold anyone offers."

Tom's clothes had been completely ruined so his mother sat down to make him some new ones. Soon he was looking smart and cheerful again. His parents gave him lots of good food and drink, and before long they had forgotten all the terrible adventures he had been through.